The Mushroom Forest

This story shows the value of self-esteem, and how friends
can help you to see yourself in a positive way.

Story by:
Phil Baron

Illustrated by:

David High
Russell Hicks
Douglas McCarthy
Allyn Conley-Gorniak
Julie Ann Armstrong

Lorann Downer
Rivka
Matthew Bates
Fay Whitemountain
Marilyn Gage

WORLDS OF WONDER™

Worlds of Wonder, Inc. is the exclusive licensee, manufacturer and distributor of The World of Teddy Ruxpin toys.
"The World of Teddy Ruxpin" and "Teddy Ruxpin" are trademarks of Alchemy II, Inc., Chatsworth, CA.
The symbol **W•W** and "Worlds of Wonder" are trademarks of Worlds of Wonder, Inc., Fremont, California.

Grubby™ Newton Gimmick™ Princess Aruzia™ Leota™ Wooly What's-It™

Prince Arin™ Fobs®

Teddy

Hi, there. Boy, I think it's too hot to tell a story today.

Grubby

Yeah, especially seein' as we're here in The Great Desert.

Teddy

That's true, Grubby.

Grubby

Gimmick thought it would be a good idea to visit The Great Desert in the summertime.

Gimmick

Yes! Well, there are some beautiful rock formations here.

Grubby

Hmmm, I wonder if they're just as beautiful in the wintertime?

Gimmick

Oh, yes! I think they probably are.

Teddy

Well, maybe if we sing a song, we'll forget how hot we are.

Grubby

Oh, no. I'm not doin' anything that'll make me hotter.

Page 1

"It's So Hot"

It's so hot,
You just wanna be lazy.
So hot,
It'll almost drive you crazy.
It's the kind of day that you
Would almost rather stay in bed.
It's the kind of day that you
Could fry an omelet on your head.

'Cause it's so hot,
It's the worst you've ever felt.
Yes, it's so hot,
That you think you're gonna melt.
It's the kind of day that's even
Hotter in the shade.
It's the kind of day you'd like to
Fill your pool with lemonade.

There's nowhere to hide.
Even inside
It's like an oven.
You know, it's so hard to bear,
The heat's everywhere.
It's even above 'n below...

So hot,
You just wanna be lazy.
So hot,
It'll almost drive you crazy.
It's the kind of day you'd rather
Stand under a hose.
It's the kind of day that you could
Light a fire with your nose.

'Cause it's so hot,
So hot, so hot.
Yes, it's so hot,
So hot, so hot.
Yes, it's so hot,
So hot, so hot.
It's so hot, yeah!

Grubby

Hey, you tricked me into singin'!

Teddy

Well, it did help us forget the heat.

Grubby

Yeah, for a minute, but now I'm even hotter than before.

Teddy

Hey, Gimmick, aren't we near the Mushroom Forest?

Gimmick

Why yes, I believe you're right, Teddy.

Teddy

And isn't the Mushroom Forest damp, dark and cool all year 'round?

Gimmick

Yes it is, Teddy. Say, I have an idea. Why don't we visit the Mushroom Forest? It's very close, and it's damp, dark and cool all year 'round!

Teddy & Grubby

Good idea, Gimmick.

Teddy

So Grubby, Newton Gimmick and I got into the airship and flew to the Mushroom Forest.

Gimmick

Okay, everyone, prepare to land!

Teddy

We landed in a small clearing in the center of the Mushroom Forest. It was damp, dark and cool. Then we got down from the airship and took a look around.

Grubby

I feel better already.

Teddy

So do I. Why don't we sit down and relax and cool off for awhile.

Gimmick

That's a good idea, Teddy. Whoops!

Grubby

What happened, Gimmick?

Gimmick

Well, I tripped over this rock. Hmmm, that's interesting.

Teddy

What is, Gimmick?

Gimmick

Well, wasn't this a rock?

Grubby

Gee, isn't that a bush, Gimmick?

Gimmick

Well it is, but it wasn't. That is to say...hmmm, this is interesting!

Teddy

Something very strange happened. Gimmick thought he tripped over a rock, but now it was a bush.

Grubby

Hmmm, maybe the heat's gettin' to us, Teddy.

Teddy

Yes, I guess so.

Grubby

Hey, these big mushrooms make good chairs! Whhhhoops!

Teddy

The mushroom Grubby was sitting on suddenly slipped out from under him!

Grubby

Hey! My chair's walkin' away!

Gimmick

What we are seeing here is scientifically impossible.

Teddy

Excuse me, Mr. or Ms. Mushroom…?

This

B-b-b-b-b-b…!

Gimmick

Don't be afraid. We won't hurt you.

Grubby

I'm sorry I sat on ya.

Teddy

Who are you?

This

I-I-I-I-I-I'm a Nothing. Nothing at all.

Teddy

The poor little creature was so frightened of us, he could barely speak.

You mean, you're not a mushroom?

This

I told you, I'm a Nothing. N-n-now leave me alone.

Grubby

What's your name, Mr. Nothin'?

This

Th-Th-Th-This.

Grubby

Huh?

Teddy

This really was a Nothing. He told us that he was one of a shy family of creatures who called themselves Nothings, because they had no shape of their own. This came in handy when they wanted to hide from danger.

Gimmick

You mean you don't always look like a mushroom?

This

Oh, n-n-n-no. We can change into almost any shape we want. Now, p-please go away.

Teddy

Where are the other Nothings?

This

O-Oh, they're hiding. They're just too sh-shy to come out. I'm the b-b...I'm the b-b-b-bravest one.

Teddy

This said he was the first Nothing to talk to anyone since his great-grandfather, Timid the Brave, said "hi" to a Fob... nearly a hundred years ago!

Gimmick

Yes! I can see that the Mushroom Forest would make an ideal home for such bashful creatures.

Grubby

I wonder if there are any more of these Nothin' guys around here.

Teddy

Just then, a beautiful flower popped right up under Grubby's nose...

Grubby

Hey!

Gimmick

Ooh, that tickles!

Teddy

...and a bush behind Gimmick started poking him in the back.

Gimmick

Now, stop that!

Teddy

Suddenly, a bunch of mushrooms jumped right up in front of me and started dancing!

Gimmick

I think we've been surrounded by Nothings all along.

Teddy

This is wonderful!

Gimmick

Hello, Nothings. Won't you come out and, and be friends?

Teddy

It's very nice to meet you.

Nothings

Likewise, we're sure.

Grubby

Hey, Gimmick, that rock ya tripped over before turned into a bush, and now it's a somethin'...I mean, a Nothin'!

That

H-H-Hello! M-My name is, is, is That.

The Other

I'm The Other.

Grubby

The Other what?

The Other

The Other N-N-Nothing.

Teddy

This, That, and The Other didn't feel so afraid now. More and more Nothings came out of hiding until we were surrounded by funny looking rocks, plants and mushrooms of every shape and size.

This

W-W-Would, w-would you, would you like to play a g-g-game with us?

Grubby

Oh boy! I'm gonna love *this!* Oops, I mean, I love games!

Teddy

Sure, *that* would be fun. Oops, I mean, it would be fun!

Gimmick

Yes, we want to get to know you, one way or *the other*...oops, I mean...yes!

This

G-G-G-Good. It's the very favorite game of Nothings. It's called "Hide and Seek."

"Hide and Seek"

Hide and seek,
Hide and seek,
It's lots of fun to play
Hide and seek.
Hide and seek,
Hide and seek,
I never get tired of
Hide and seek.

Not it!
Not it!
Not it!
Not it! Gee, I guess I'm it.

ONE...
You lean against a tree.
TWO...
Start counting one, two, three,

THREE...
While everyone goes running
FOUR...
Off to hide somewhere.
FIVE...
You cover up your eyes
SIX...
So we will realize
SEVEN...
That you're not peeking, 'cause

EIGHT...
That just would not be fair.
NINE...
Hide and seek,
Hide and seek,
TEN...
It's lots of fun to play
Hide and seek.
ELEVEN...

Hide and seek,
Hide and seek,
TWELVE...
We never get tired of
Hide and seek.
THIRTEEN...
I found a place to hide.
FOURTEEN...
I found a place to hide.
Hey, how much higher am I gonna have
    to count?
TWENTY!
Oh.
SIXTEEN...
You cover up your eyes

SEVENTEEN...
So we will realize
EIGHTEEN...
That you're not peeking,
NINETEEN...
Then you count the right amount.
TWENTY!
Ready or not, here I come.
Hide and seek is lots of fun.

Dum dee dum,
Dum dee do,
Dum dee doodly,
Dum dee dee.

Ooo, hoo, I see Gimmick hiding
Behind the rock!

FREE!
Golly, Gimmick, I didn't
Know ya could run that fast!

Here I come!
Dum dee dum...
I thought it was fun to play
Hide and seek.

Oh, hey, wait a minute, Teddy!
Wait!
FREE!
Aw, gee, Teddy.

You guys just run too fast.
You beat me to the tree.
Now where do you suppose
The Nothin's all could be?

They must be here somewhere.
Well, I'm not sure that's fair.
I think they changed their shapes
Around to just fool me.
I give up. I give up.
Ollie-ollie-all-in-free!
Here we are! Here we are!
They're standin' right next to me.

Hide and seek,
Hide and seek,
Nothings are good at
Hide and seek.
Hide and seek,
Hide and seek,
It's lots of fun to play
Hide and seek.
Hide and seek,
Hide and seek,
It's lots of fun to play

Hide and seek.
Hide and seek,
Hide and seek,
We never get tired of
Hide and seek.

HIDE AND SEEK!

Teddy

After playing hide and seek, the Nothings put on a wonderful show for us...changing into a hundred different shapes and colors...right before our eyes!

Grubby

This is sure fun! Hey, how about turnin' into somethin' to eat. I'm gettin' hungry!

Teddy

Grubby!

Grubby

Just kiddin'.

Teddy

Do you always live here in the Mushroom Forest?

This, That & The Other
Ah, w-we didn't use to, b-b-but i-it's easier to hide here where i-i-it's dark. B-Besides, mushrooms are easy to imitate.

Gimmick
You know, Teddy, these fellows are really amazing.

Teddy
I agree, Gimmick. I don't think you should call yourselves "Nothings" anymore.

This
But, but that's what we are.

Teddy
But since you can become anything you want, I think you should call yourselves…"ANYTHINGS"!

"You Are An Anything"

You're not a Nothing.
You are an Anything!
How high you learn to fly
Is how wide you spread your wings.

You're not a Nothing.
You are an Anything!
The world is out there waiting now
To hear the song you sing.

Just do your best.
Use your imagination.
Stand up to the test.
You've got lots of inspiration.

There's nothing in the world
You shouldn't try to do,
'Cause there's no one more
Magnificent than you.

You're not a Nothing.
You are an Anything!
So, don't be timid,
Don't be shy,
Don't just watch the world go by.

You're not a Nothing.
You are an Anything!
So, put a sparkle in your eye.
Good things happen when you try.

Make up your mind.
There's nothing to frighten you,
And soon you will find
That ya like the things ya do.

Be anything at all
That you should want to be.
There's one enormous world
Out there for you to see.

We're not a Nothing.
We are an Anything.
How high you learn to fly
Is how wide you spread your wings.

We're not a Nothing.
We are an Anything.
The world is out there waiting now
To hear the song we sing.

The world is out there waiting now
To hear the song you sing.

This

G-Gee, with good friends like you, I don't feel like a Nothing anymore.

The Other

I like our new name. We're Anythings!

Anythings

We're Anythings! Yippi!

Gimmick

Teddy, we should be getting on our way now.

This

O-Oh, but Teddy, before you go we'd like to make you, Grubby and Gimmick honorary Anythings.

Grubby

But we can't turn into mushrooms and stuff like you can.

This

Oh, I know, but you can be anything you want.

Teddy

Thank you, all.

This, That & The Other

And we learned to be two things that we never were b-before. We learned to be brave, and we learned to b-b-be friends!

We're not a Nothing.
We are an Anything!
How high you learn to fly
Is how wide you spread your wings.

We're not a Nothing.
We are an Anything!
The world is out there waiting now
To hear the song we sing.

The world is out there waiting now
To hear the song you sing.